# ALL ASLEEP

## BY CHARLOTTE POMERANTZ

## ILLUSTRATED BY NANCY TAFURI

PUFFIN BOOKS

# FOR CARLO
—C.P.

# FOR MILTON
—N.T.

PUFFIN BOOKS
Viking Penguin Inc., 40 West 23rd Street, New York, New York 10010, U.S.A.
Penguin Books Ltd, Harmondsworth, Middlesex, England
Penguin Books Australia Ltd, Ringwood, Victoria, Australia
Penguin Books Canada Limited, 2801 John Street, Markham, Ontario, Canada L3R 1B4
Penguin Books (N.Z.) Ltd, 182-190 Wairau Road, Auckland 10, New Zealand

First published by Greenwillow Books 1984
Published in Picture Puffins 1986

Text copyright © Charlotte Pomerantz, 1984
Illustrations copyright © Nancy Tafuri, 1984
All rights reserved

Printed in U.S.A.
by Rae Publishing Co., Inc., Cedar Grove, New Jersey

Library of Congress Cataloging in Publication Data
Pomerantz, Charlotte.    All asleep.
Summary: A collection of lullabies and other poems suitable for reading at bedtime.
1. Sleep—Juvenile poetry.    2. Lullabies.    3. Children's poetry, American.
[1. Sleep—Poetry.    2. Lullabies.    3. Bedtime—Poetry.    4. American poetry]
I. Tafuri, Nancy, ill.    II. Title.
PS3566.0538A8    1986    811′ .54    85-43128    ISBN 0-14-050548-2

# CONTENTS

## ALL ASLEEP–I

A lamb has a lambkin,
A duck has a duckling,
And I have a baby,
Good night,
Good night,
I have a baby,
Good night.

An owl has an owlet,
A pig has a suckling,
And I have a baby,
Good night,
Sleep tight,
I have a baby,
Good night.

Even a frog
Has a wee polliwog,
And I have a baby,
Star light,
Star bright,
I have a baby.
Good night.

# THE PUPPY'S SONG

With my short legs dragging
And my long ears drooping
And my tail not wagging
And my nose not snooping,

I can't be sleepy, cause I just woke up.
No, I can't be sleepy, cause I'm just a pup.
So why don't I feel like running about?

Think I'll take a little snoozle
And then find out.

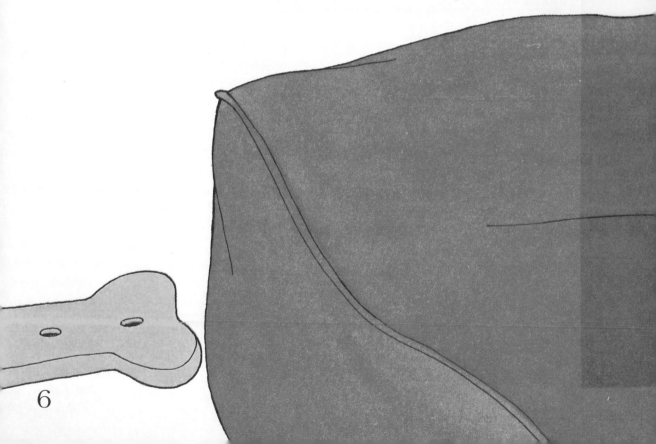

# MOON BOAT

Moon Boat, little, brave and bright,
Tossed upon the seas of night,
One day when I'm free to roam,
I'll climb aboard and steer you home.

# DROWSY BEES

The drowsy bumbling bumblebee
And the humming humblebee,
Are, as you will plainly see,
The selfsame busy buzzy bee.

For the bumbling bumblebee
Is always humming drowsily,
While the humming humblebee
Bumbles oh so bumbily.

Therefore, since the bumble hums,
He is called a humblebee;
Likewise, since the humble bums,
He is called a bumblebee.

Unless, of course, these be shee-bees;
Wherefore, to put them at their ease,
You'd call them humble bumble shees,
Or humble drowsy bumble shees.

That way, you'd be sure to p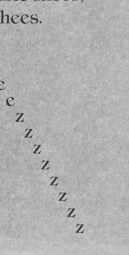

10

# ROLL GENTLY,
# OLD DUMP TRUCK
**(may be sung to the tune of "Flow Gently, Sweet Afton")**

Roll gently, old dump truck,
Through dark city streets
Piled high with cracked eggshells
And leftover beets.

My Daniel's asleep
But he's dreaming of you.
Disturb not my Daniel
When you're rumbling through.

There a toaster, a TV,
A split baseball bat,
A child's old dump truck
Whose tires are flat.

But Daniel's toy dump truck
Is shiny and new.
So please do not take it
When you're rumbling through.

12

# GRANDPA'S LULLABY

(note: Ninna-nanna means singsong or
lullaby in "children's" Italian)

I've sung you, ninna-nanna,
Seven singsong lullabies.
I've begged you, ninna-nanna,
To be still and close your eyes.

I've kissed you, ninna-nanna,
And I've hugged you very tight;
But I will not sing you
One more ninna-nanna song tonight.

So darling, ninna-nanna,
Let me make it clear to you,
That if you do not go to sleep
At once, here's what I'll do:

I'll trim off all your dolly's
Fluffy ninna-nanna hair.
I'll paddywhack the bottom
Of your ninna-nanna bear.

14

I'll take the copper pennies
From your ninna-nanna jar,
And buy myself a ninna-nanna
Nifty candy bar.

I'll let your tweet-tweet parakeet
Go flying roundabout,
Then open up the white mouse house
And let the white mouse out.

For grandpa is so tired
He could fall down in a heap.
I cannot stay awake. . . .
But what's this—you're fast asleep!

# DON'T MAKE A PEEP

Hush, my chicks, don't make a peep.
Soon you will be fast asleep.

*What if we do make a peep?*
*Look at us—we're not asleep.*

Mm, I must agree, peep-peep.
Clearly you are not asleep.

*No, we're not, we're not asleep.*
*We are wide awake, peep-peep.*

What clever chicks you are, peep-peep.
You've found a way to never sleep.

*Hooray, hooray. We'll never sleep.*
*All night long, we'll peep-peep-peep.*

Whyever did I let you peep?
Now you'll never, ever sleep.

*Never sleep, peep-peep-peep-peep.*
*Not ever sleep, peep-peep-peep-peep.*
*All night long, peep-peep-peep-peep.*
*Never. Ever. Go to sleeeeeeeeee*

# HUSH, MY POSY SLEEPS

Hush, my Posy sleeps
In the grassy deeps.
The moo cows moo,
The love doves coo,
While my Posy sleeps.

Hush, my Posy dreams
Of bubbly moonlit streams,
Where seabells ring
And mermaids sing—
While my Posy sleeps.

# GRANDMA'S LULLABY

Close your eyes,
My precious love,
Grandma's little
Turtledove.

Go to sleep now,
Pretty kitty,
Grandma's little
Chickabiddy.

Stop your crying,
Cuddly cutie,
Grandma's little
Sweet patootie.

Issum, wissum,
Popsy wopsy,
Tootsie wootsie
Lollypopsie.
Diddims
Huggle
Snuggle pup

And now, for Grandma's sake, hush up!

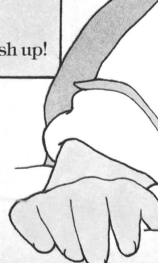

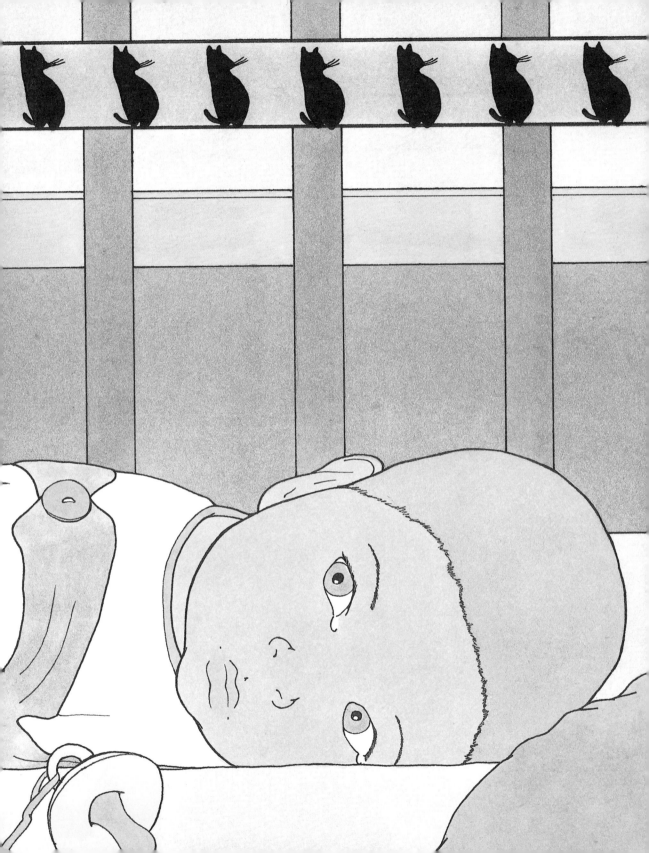

# FROG'S LULLABY

Sleep, my pretty polliwog,
Polly wolly wiggle wog

Polly wiggle waggle wog
Wiggle waggle woggle wog

Polly wolly wiggle waggle
Wiggle waggle woggle froggle

Sleep, my little wiggle head,
In your little water bed.

Sweet dreams, pretty polliwog.
When you wake, you'll be a frog.

# THE HALF LULLABY

I know a young fellow
(The story is true),

Who has one of a thing;
He does not want two.

One earmuff, one shoelace,
One raggedy mitten;

One work boot, one cufflink,
One letter, half-written;

One chopstick, one slipper,
One sock that needs mending,

And a half lullaby
Without any ending

# LITTLE BROTHER
# PUTS HIS DOLL TO SLEEP
(with the help of big sister)

Sleepy dolly, rest your head.
It is time to go to sleep.

*No, no, no. Not sleep, but <u>bed</u>.*
*It is time to go to bed.*

Oh.
It is time to go to bed
And rest your tired little—feet?

*No, no, no. Not feet, but <u>head</u>.*
*Rest your tired little head.*

Oh.
Rest your tired little head.
I'll bring you milk and ginger—snaps?

*No, no, no. Not snaps, but <u>bread</u>.*
*I'll bring you milk and gingerbread.*

Oh.
I'll bring you milk and gingerbread.
And now it's time to go to—sleep?

*No!*

Okay, <u>okay</u>. Not sleep, but bed.
Now it's time to go to bed.

*Yes, yes, yes! It's time for bed.*
*Good night, honey.*
*Good night, dolly.*
*What's your dolly's name?*

It's Molly.
Jolly Molly is my dolly.
She rides on a tiny trolly.

*Oh my gosh and oh gee whiz!*

Uh-uh. Not gee whiz, but golly.
Oh my gosh and oh my golly.

# THE PUFFIN

Warm and plump as fresh-baked muffins
Sleep the downy little puffins
Nestling in their puffinry
On cliffs that overhang the sea.

Above, a lark, a winging gull.
Below, the ever-rolling sea.
Through the lull, the singing dark,
The puffins hear the rolling sea.
The sea, the ever-rolling sea.

A puffin sniffles, starts to cry,
"Mommy, daddy, why can't I
Dive for fish way down below?"

"No," they say, "first sleep and grow.
And if you sleep, you'll get your wish."

So puffin slept—and dreamed of fish.

# THE RUMBLY NIGHT TRAIN

I cross the old bridge
In fog and in rain.
I cross the old bridge
On the rumbly night train.

I look for my dream
On the bridge where I found it
And then, alas, lost it
In fog and in rain.

And so I keep crossing
And crossing and crossing
For deep is my longing
To dream it again.

Some night I'll find
My dream on the bridge
And take it with me
On the rumbly night train.

And then I'll cross back,
Holding tight to my dream,
And when I cross over,
I'll dream it again.

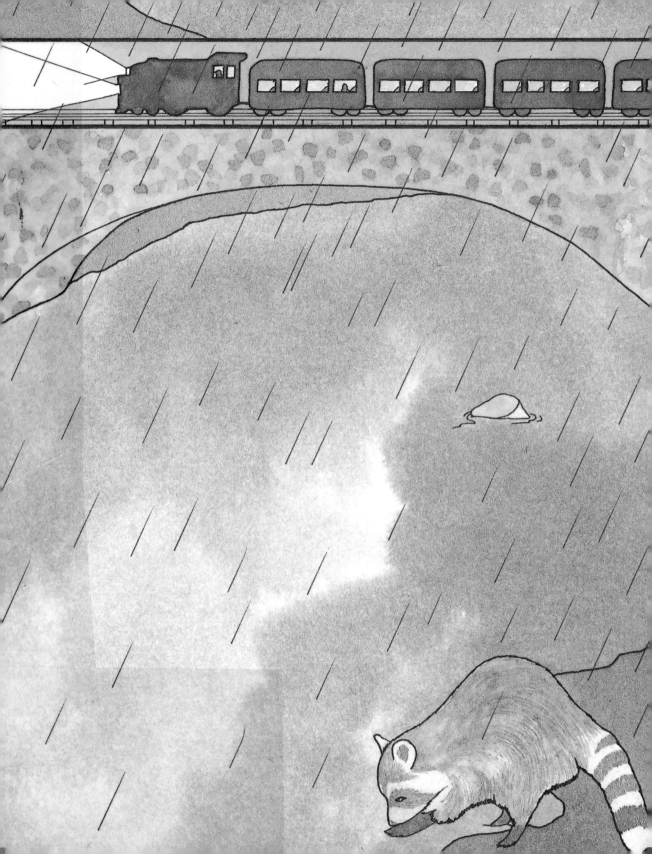

# ALL ASLEEP-II

Hush, it's the hour
When all little babies—
The lambkin,
The duckling,
The owlet,
The suckling,
Even the polliwog
Of the frog,

All little babies
And my little baby,
Close their eyes
And nod their heads,
In fields and ponds,
In tiny beds,

and sleep.